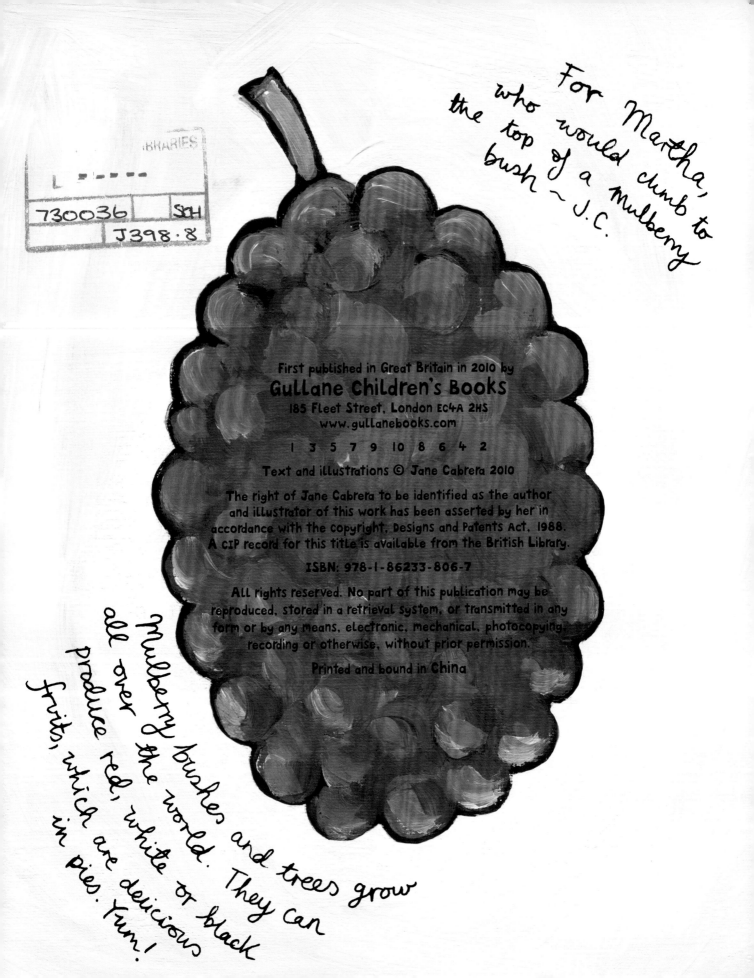

For Martha,
who would climb to
the top of a Mulberry
bush ~ J.C.

First published in Great Britain in 2010 by

Gullane Children's Books

185 Fleet Street, London EC4A 2HS
www.gullanebooks.com

1 3 5 7 9 10 8 6 4 2

Text and illustrations © Jane Cabrera 2010

The right of Jane Cabrera to be identified as the author
and illustrator of this work has been asserted by her in
accordance with the copyright, Designs and Patents Act, 1988.
A CIP record for this title is available from the British Library.

ISBN: 978-1-86233-806-7

Printed and bound in China

Mulberry bushes and trees grow
all over the world. They can
produce red, white or black
fruits, which are delicious
in pies. Yum!

Here We Go Round the Mulberry Bush

Jane Cabrera

GULLANE
CHILDREN'S BOOKS

This is the way we all **wake up**,
All **wake up**, all **wake up**.

This is the way we all **wake up**,
On a cold and frosty morning.

This is the way we **brush** our teeth,
Brush our teeth, **brush** our teeth.
This is the way we **brush** our teeth,
On a cold and frosty morning.

This is the way we all **get dressed,**
All **get dressed,** all **get dressed.**

This is the way we all **get dressed,**
On a cold and frosty morning.

This is the way we **march** to school,
March to school, **march** to school.

This is the way we **march** to school,
On a cold and frosty morning.

Here we go round
the mulberry bush,
The mulberry bush, the mulberry bush,
Here we go round the mulberry bush,
On a cold and frosty morning.

This is the way we **read** and **write**,
Read and **write**, **read** and **write**.

This is the way we **read** and **write**,
On a cold and frosty afternoon.

This is the way we **jump** and **skip**,
Jump and **skip**, **jump** and **skip**.

This is the way we **jump** and **skip**,
On a cold and frosty afternoon.

This is the way we hop **home** from school,
Home from school, **home** from school.
This is the way we hop **home** from school,
On a cold and frosty afternoon.

This is the way we bounce **up** and **down**.
Up and **down**, **up** and **down**.
This is the way we bounce **up** and **down**,

On a cold and frosty evening.

This is the way we **splash** about,
Splash about, **splash** about.

This is the way we **splash** about,
On a cold and frosty evening.

This is the way we **settle down,**
Settle down, settle down.

This is the way we **settle down**,
On a cold and frosty evening.

This is the way we go to **sleep**,
Go to **sleep**, go to **sleep**.

This is the way we go to **sleep**,
On a cold and frosty evening.

Goodnight!